Myth Quest

Banasura

THE THOUSAND-ARMED ASURA

retold by Anu Kumar

illustrations by Amir Khan

First published in 2012 by Hachette India
(Registered name: Hachette Book Publishing India Pvt. Ltd)
An Hachette UK company
www.hachetteindia.com

SRD

ISBN 978-93-5009-534-8

Hachette Book Publishing India Pvt Ltd,
4th & 5th Floors, Corporate Centre;
Plot No. 94, Sector 44; Gurgaon 122003, India

Typeset in Adobe Garamond Pro 13/16
by Eleven Arts, New Delhi

Printed and bound in India by
Manipal Technologies Limited, Manipal

Welcome to the world of MythQuest...

Discover the fables and legends about the origin, history, deities, ancestors and heroes of India.

While the term 'myth' in common conversation means a false story, in the world of religion, folklore and magic, myths are considered 'true'. They tell stories of the creation of the universe, the eternal battle between good and evil and the history of humankind itself.

The main characters in our myths are bigger and better than any modern superheroes. They are birds and beasts, asuras and gods, kings and queens, generals and warriors, sages and gurus, each with extraordinary powers that changed the course of history and the fate of the human race.

The people to whom a myth belongs consider it as a true account of their past millions of years ago. Even today, they continue to worship the gods and goddesses, follow the rituals and read the texts that developed from these myths.

Hachette India's MythQuest series brings to you fascinating stories from the vast treasures of ancient mythology. Read them all—become a MythMaster!

Mythological characters and events have been described in different ways in different versions of ancient texts. We have chosen the most interesting and key stories to build a comprehensive account for the young reader.

This story is about . . .

Banasura, the thousand-armed asura. *He was the son of the great* asura *king, Mahabali or Bali. Banasura was an ardent devotee of Lord Shiva, the Destroyer of the Universe, and spent many years in penance to please Shiva. Pleased by his devotion, Lord Shiva blessed Banasura and promised to come to his assistance whenever he was challenged in battle.*

Banasura's daughter Usha fell in love with Lord Krishna's grandson, Aniruddha, following which, a great battle ensued between Lord Krishna and the asura *king. This battle was recounted far and wide, for in it, Lord Shiva fought against Lord Krishna.*

Unlike his father, Bali, who was one of the most benevolent and generous asura *kings loved by all, Banasura chose the path of terror and optressed the inhabitants of all three worlds.*

Banasura or Bana's story has been told in ancient texts including the Bhagavata Purana and the Mahabharata. His story as the rejected suitor of Shakti, has also been mentioned in the great Tamil Sangam literary works Manimekalai and Puranaanooru. Read about his super weapons and his battles against the mighty gods . . .

CHAPTER ONE

LORD SHIVA'S PROMISE

The earth shuddered, streaks of lightening tore through the skies, the mountains echoed with the sound of thunder, and all the creatures in the universe trembled—Lord Shiva, the Destroyer of the Universe, was dancing his *tandava*, the dance of creation, preservation and dissolution. He flung his arms out and stomped the ground with his powerful feet. He performed his steps with lightning speed and was so fast that the celestial musicians just couldn't keep up with him. One by one the musicians gave up in exhaustion, until only one was left—Banasura the thousand-armed *asura*.

Banasura used his many arms to play every kind of instrument for Lord Shiva, long after others had stopped. When he would grow tired of one instrument, he would lay it aside and start playing something else. Banasura's melodious tunes filled every corner of the

universe. Lord Shiva was enchanted by these notes and when he finally stopped dancing, he looked down to see who was playing the music.

His gaze fell upon Banasura and he smiled at him. Banasura's joy knew no bounds. Shiva was the one god who was very hard to please and the *asura* had done just that. However, Banasura's presence and his musical performance was no accident. It was all part of an elaborate plan that he had hatched.

This was no ordinary *asura*. He was the son of the legendary Bali, the great *asura* king, grandson of Prahlada, to whom Lord Vishnu, Preserver of the Universe, had himself promised his protection. Bali was a wise and just king. He was also invincible because of a boon granted to him by Lord Brahma, Creator of the Universe. He not only conquered all the kingdoms on earth and the nether regions, but also Heaven, forcing Indra, the King of Gods into exile. Bali's ambition frightened the gods. They appealed to Lord Vishnu to get Heaven back from Bali and restore the balance in the universe. Thus Lord Vishnu had appeared in the form of a dwarf, Vamana. And in the midst of all his courtiers and guests, Vamana tricked Bali into giving up his kingdom. Not only was Bali stripped of his kingdoms, he was also humiliated and finally pushed into the underworld as Vamana placed one giant leg on his head. However because of his kindness, he was made king of the underworld and allowed to visit his people on earth once a year.

Banasura was the eldest of Bali's hundred sons. As a young boy, he had been at the great sacrifice that

his father had held and he clearly remembered how Bali had been humiliated in his own court, surrounded by the most accomplished men and respected guests. He was determined that someday he would get back the three realms over which his father held sway.

Now, Banasura was a great devotee of Lord Shiva and spent hours in penance and meditation. He was determined to seek the blessings of Shiva, knowing that if Shiva was on his side, the gods would not oppose him and he would achieve his goal.

And so when Shiva expressed his pleasure at the music he played, he was overjoyed.

'Banasura,' Shiva's deep voice boomed. 'You have pleased me with your perseverance and devotion. You have my blessings. You may seek your heart's desire from me.'

This was the moment the Banasura had been waiting for. Bowing low, and very humbly folding all his thousand arms, he made his request.

'O powerful god, promise me that from now on, you will be my protector. And each time I am challenged in battle, you will come to my aid if I call you.'

Shiva nodded his great head. 'It shall be as you wish.'

'And O Lord, promise me that you will guard the gates of my city Sonitapur. The entire universe trembles at the very sight of you. And with you at my gates I shall be safe. I beg you to accept my humble request.'

Now Lord Shiva realized what these requests meant. He saw that Banasura was filled with ambition and he wanted to get back his father's power and kingdom. Shiva also understood that the *asura* was using his godly powers to achieve his ambition. The god swelled with rage at this realization, but once he had offered to grant a boon, he could not take it back. So he promised that he would come to Banasura's assistance whenever required; but he would not be Banasura's gatekeeper.

Before he left, however, Shiva warned Banasura, 'One day you will meet a formidable warrior, who will break your flagstaff and challenge your power. This warrior will best you in any contest and defeat any weapon that you might send his way. You must be prepared for that humiliation. This will mark the end of your days as a great *asura* king.'

The flagstaff, displaying the symbol of the king and his dynasty, is placed at the gate of a king's palace. If someone breaks it, it is seen as an insult and a challenge to the king. Banasura dreamt of his flagstaff towering high and visible from afar, a symbol of his supremacy over the world. He felt sure that with Lord Shiva on his side, no one would dare touch the staff and oppose him. He thought himself invincible and in his arrogance, he refused to heed Shiva's warning.

Before long, he expanded his kingdom and ruled over a vast land. So strong and fierce was his influence, that all the kings and even the gods looked on with alarm at his growing power. Banasura only grew worse over time and the added power gave an edge to his cruel ways.

This evil asura tyrannized his poor subjects. Neighbouring kings had no chance against his might and humans and lesser *asuras* cowered in fear when he approached. He wiped out whole kingdoms and made many kings his slaves, as he embarked upon his grand plan to rule the universe. No one could stand up to him. Even Lord Shiva grew worried seeing the effects of the boon he had granted.

Meanwhile, Banasura's wickedness continued unchecked and even extended to his own family. His lovely daughter, Usha was also subject to her father's cruelties and imprisoned for no fault of her own.

CHAPTER TWO

PRINCESS USHA'S DREAM

Banasura had a daughter called Usha. She was a vision of beauty. Suitors came from far and wide to ask for her hand. Banasura, however, refused them all. Instead, he had her imprisoned in a fortress called Agnigarh to keep her away from all the men, *asuras* and gods who might want to woo her. True to its name, the fort was surrounded by great flames of fire and a posse of guards maintained a round-the-clock vigil.

Usha's only companion during her imprisonment, was her devoted friend Chitralekha. She was the daughter of Kusamanda, one of Banasura's most trusted ministers.

One night, as Usha slept, a young man appeared in her dreams. He was so handsome and charming that she couldn't help but fall in love with him. When she woke up, Usha was excited and eagerly told Chitralekha about her dream. 'Chitralekha, I would give anything to know who the young man is. But there is no way to find out, since my father has me watched at all times,' she confided.

Chitralekha and Usha had grown to be very close friends. Having heard her story, Chitralekha felt very sorry for her. Locked up in this heavily guarded palace, it was impossible for Usha to escape and find her love. Chitralekha thought deeply over the matter. If there was a way, Chitralekha would help Usha attain her heart's desire. She thought for a while and soon, she had a plan to help her friend.

Now Chitralekha was a wise and clever woman. She had many talents and was a wonderfully accomplished artist with a vivid imagination. She had the guards secretly deliver palm leaves for her to paint on. And then, over several days and nights, she drew portraits of every handsome god, prince and demi-god she could think of. As she drew them, she showed them to Usha so that she could pick out the man in her dreams.

Her nimble fingers sketched a figure, which she then filled with her bright colours to produce a lovely life-like image. And after each figure was completed, she would ask Usha, 'Is he the one?'

She drew Lord Indra, the King of Gods and Lord of Heaven. She sketched Lord Brahma, the Creator of the Universe, and many other *devas,* or gods, but Usha shook her head. None of these figures resembled the prince who had appeared in her dream.

Finally, Chitralekha drew a portrait of Lord Krishna's grandson, Aniruddha. Usha took one look at it and drew her breath. She looked at Chitralekha and smiled shyly at her. Chitralekha immediately knew that this was the prince Usha had lost her heart to.

Chitralekha thought hard about what she should do next. Identifying the man of Usha's dreams was wonderful, but a far greater task lay head. Aniruddha was Krishna's grandson and he lived, as did all the other Yadavas, in Dwarka which was far to the west, while Sonitapur was in the east. How would she be able to arrange a meeting between the two? Also how could Usha break free of her prison?

Chitralekha knew it would be hard to reach Aniruddha. But she had some mystical powers and so chanting some special prayers she had learnt, she made herself lighter than a feather and was soon flying high towards the sky. Sitting on a cloud, she flew a long distance across the land and when she reached Dwarka it was already very dark. Fortunately, it was also a very peaceful night, so everyone including the guards, had fallen asleep.

Obviously no one was expecting a mysterious woman who flew through the skies. And so, Chitralekha dropped to the ground effortlessly, and then crept past windows, without encountering any opposition. Noiseless as a bird, she crept into the innermost chambers where the Yadava princes slept.

She spotted Aniruddha asleep and he was just as Usha had dreamed. She could not fault her friend's choice. And now, determined to carry out her plan, she made herself stronger, lifted the cot with the sleeping Aniruddha lying on it and flew all the way back with him.

Since she had travelled across the land, it was once more night when she reached Sonitapur. So she was able to slip in unnoticed. And then feeling more than a little pleased with herself, she presented Aniruddha to her friend. And just as she did, Aniruddha woke up. Although it had been a long journey from Dwarka, Aniruddha had been peacefully asleep and now he woke looking as fresh and handsome as if he had woken in his own palace.

He looked around him in great surprise. 'Where am I? How did I get here?' he wondered aloud. This was not his own palace. It was a place he had never seen before. And instead of his attendants, he found two women staring down at him. One of them looked at him fixedly and blushed even as she stared—she was the most beautiful woman he had ever laid eyes upon.

And as it had been willed in Usha's dream, Aniruddha too fell in love with her at first sight and wished to marry her. 'If you so wish I will perform your marriage rituals,' said Chitralekha. And when the young couple nodded, she said, 'However, this marriage will have to be a secret one, for everyone knows that Banasura hates Krishna and will never accept this union.'

Usha and Aniruddha agreed, and using her special powers, Chitralekha married them in the *gandharva* style, which was one of seven kinds of marriage permitted in the ancient times, when two people wished to marry each other in utter secrecy.

It was of utmost importance that the marriage remained a secret, for Banasura truly hated Krishna as he was an incarnation of Lord Vishnu. Vishnu in his incarnation as Narasimha, had killed Banasura's ancestors, Hiranyakashipu and Hiranyaksha; and in the guise of Vamana, he had humiliated Banasura's father, Bali.

Aniruddha and Usha spent several blissful days together in the palace, but it was not long before Banasura's spies brought the *asura* king news of a handsome stranger who had been seen in his daughter's closely guarded palace.

Banasura's anger knew no bounds. 'Who dares to enter my daughter's palace? Find him and bring him to me in chains!' he roared.

He sent a few of his bravest and most capable soldiers to the fort to capture Aniruddha.

Aniruddha was taken by surprise. Yet, he was no ordinary young man and put up a brave fight. He was after all, grandson of the great Lord Krishna, who had battled *asuras* and *rakshasas* and fought many great wars in order to rid the world of evil. Aniruddha's father was the great hero, Pradyumna, who had defeated the evil demon, Sambara and won many accolades in battle. Coming from such a great lineage, it was natural that Aniruddha would also show great prowess in the arts of war.

He managed to wrest an iron mace out of the hands of one of the demons and with it, he clubbed the nearest ones on their head and knocked them out cold. He went at some others with his bare fists and wrestled two of them to the ground at the same time.

Seeing that this was not turning out too well, one of Banasura's men ran back to the *asura* king's palace to inform him and get reinforcements. Enraged at the gall of the young prince, Banasura let out a huge bellow and then himself ran to the fortress with a dozen of his best warriors.

Even though Aniruddha was unarmed, he put up a brave fight. However, Banasura was extremely strong and wielded different weapons in each of his thousand arms. His men were also very strong and there were many of them. They easily outnumbered him and began to close in on him. But Aniruddha did not give up so easily. He valiantly resisted Banasura's men, but was unable to withstand the onslaught of blows from the *asura* king himself. Bleeding and exhausted, in the end, he was beaten to the ground.

All this while Usha watched helplessly from the sidelines. She now fell weeping at her father's feet, begging for her husband's life. However, it was to no avail. Banasura had him bound with snakes, and imprisoned in the deepest dungeons of his palace. Banasura's dungeons were the stuff of nightmares, crawling with rats and other creatures of the night. It was a place of total darkness from where Aniruddha couldn't even see the light of day. Here, the Yadava prince languished in chains, hoping for a ray of light. Even though he lived in the worst conditions, he knew in his heart, that his grandfather, Lord Krishna, would eventually find him and rescue him from his plight.

CHAPTER THREE

KRISHNA'S GREAT ANGER

Meanwhile, the next morning in Dwarka, there was chaos. Aniruddha was nowhere to be found. At first, the palace guards, courtiers, friends and relatives were unperturbed; they assumed he had gone on a hunting trip with his friends and would return in a few days.

However, the very next day, the rainy season began and continued for weeks. The torrential rains washed away roads and the fields were flooded. Horses and bullocks could barely make their way through the mud. So Aniruddha's family thought the prince's return might have been hampered by the rains; they waited and waited for the rains to pass. Yet, four months went by and there was still no sign of Aniruddha, or any lessening of the rain.

By now, the entire Yadava clan was extremely worried, especially since Krishna was away and they could not turn to him for advice. They sent out messengers, even soldiers in disguise, to discreetly find out if he had been

noticed in other cities in their neighbouring kingdoms. But they returned with no news. They all wrung their hands in despair and desperation as Aniruddha had simply disappeared!

Finally, Krishna returned from his long journey. 'And how is my grandson Aniruddha?' he asked soon after he arrived in the capital. His family immediately hung their heads in sorrow and recounted their woes. 'O Krishna, one night before the great rains began, Aniruddha disappeared. We have searched high and low for him, but have not succeeded in locating him. O Lord, now it is all up to you to do something.'

Seeing their crestfallen faces, Krishna did not berate them for having waited so long to inform him. He knew something had to be done fast.

Soon after the return of Krishna, Narada, the all-knowing, ever-travelling, heavenly bard came to visit Krishna at Dwarka. Narada had spies and gossips everywhere, who kept him informed of all the happenings in the universe. He received news from every corner of the universe—from the largest kingdoms to small secret places which no one had even seen.

The Yadavas turned to him with relief. If anyone could have news of Aniruddha's whereabouts, it would be Narada. And Narada did not disappoint. Jangling his cymbals, chanting the name of Lord Vishnu, of whom he was a great devotee, he told them all that he knew.

'Your grandson, Lord Krishna, is now a captive in Banasura's kingdom. He's locked up in the *asura's* deepest dungeons, a place so hard to reach, that even the bravest warrior would find it daunting.'

Narada went on to tell Krishna the whole story of Aniruddha's disappearance, of Usha's dream, of Chitralekha's drawing and how she had flown the entire distance to take Aniruddha back with her to fulfill her friend's desire. He told them of Banasura's fury when he was told of his daughter's liaison with a Yadava prince and finally how he had the prince captured and imprisoned for ever.

Krishna's face grew dark with anger as Narada narrated his story and he made a quick decision. Aniruddha had to be rescued and the only way to do this was to go to war.

'My brave warriors, Banasura has dared to imprison a son of Dwarka. We have to rescue him and show Banasura that we will not tolerate this insult. Prepare for war!'

All the Yadava clans immediately responded to Krishna's call and came together in this hour of crisis. And in no time at all, a huge army gathered and set forth on the long arduous journey to Banasura's kingdom.

It was a long and difficult journey from Dwarka in the west to Sonitapur in the east. The army marched across the rocky plateau of central India, crossed broad rivers and dense forests that led up to Sonitapur. They crossed the kingdoms of Vidarbha, Magadha and Gaur as well as the immense Brahmaputra River, before they finally reached Sonitapur.

Once they reached Sonitapura, this large army of Yadavas ranged itself around its boundaries. And to those who saw it, it was a fearsome sight. It was made up of 18 military divisions and in its ranks were soldiers, elephants, horses and chariots. Practically all the leaders of the family, including Pradyumna, Satyaki, Gada, Samba, Sarana, Nanda, Upananda and Bhadra had come together for the battle.

Banasura's soldiers and lookouts noticed the huge army massing at its boundaries. Although they were well armed and numerous, the *asuras* were unprepared for the ferociousness of the assault. At one signal from Krishna, the Yadava soldiers launched themselves upon the gates of Sonitapur. They aimed arrows at the towers, hurled spears at the guards and charged at the immense gates with no thought to their own safety. The great war had begun.

CHAPTER FOUR

THE GREAT WAR BEGINS

Krishna was at the helm of the Yadava army. He looked resplendent in his shining armour and fine chariot, as he cut a swathe though the ranks on the battlefield to arrive at the gates of Sonitapur. He saw Banasura's flag flying proudly in the wind, high up on the ramparts of his fort. He pulled out an arrow from his quiver and took aim. Within seconds, the flagstaff lay in pieces on the ground. Krishna had thrown down the gauntlet.

Banasura's guards were aghast. They rushed into the palace to inform him of Krishna's challenge. Banasura immediately instructed his army to retaliate. Banasura was also quite pleased with the challenge. He realized that in this battle, he was up against the powerful Yadavas and their brave warriors, led by none other than Krishna.

He knew that if he won this battle, everyone would acknowledge him as the most powerful king that ever ruled. So he set out to fight, his heart pounding in anticipation. Not once did Banasura doubt his own powers. He was sure of victory,

because he knew that he had Lord Shiva's promise on his side.

Meanwhile, the Yadavas were unrelenting. They had already damaged the strong fort walls and the

tall towers that overlooked the vast lands. Banasura was enraged!

'Take your positions and launch your attack!' he bellowed. Some of his men ran up to the ramparts. Others poured out of the gates. Barely had they taken their positions, than another army joined them. This army was led by none other than Lord Shiva with a force like no other. In the lead was Shiva, riding his loyal bull Nandi, and accompanied by his son, Kartikeya. Following him was a strange and terrifying assortment of beings, including ghosts, ghouls, spirits, vampires, and other beings who were variously called *Pretas*, *Pramathas*, *Guhyakas*, *Dakinis*, *Pisacas*, *Kusmandas*, *Vetalas*, *Vinayakas* and *Brahma-rakshasas*. These were all the creatures of the night, who hung around at cremation grounds and graveyards. They were Shiva's followers or *ganas*, ready to do his bidding at a single nod.

The battle began in right earnest. It was waged so fiercely and was so unrelenting that the other gods came to watch. The skies darkened, and the whole universe was filled with the sounds of destruction as shields and swords clashed and arrows breezed with the force of a gale.

Lord Shiva commanded Banasura's armies, his bull Nandi snorting ferociously, as he charged at Lord Krishna at the helm of the Yadava armies. Pradyumna, Krishna's son, fought against Kartikeya and Balarama,

Krishna's elder brother battled with his mace against Banasura's brave minister and general, Kumbhanda and his second-in-command, Kupakarna. Samba, one of Krishna's sons from his wife Satyabhama, clashed with Banasura's son, while Banasura himself took on the trusted friend of Krishna and formidable Yadava warrior, Satyaki.

Satyaki was especially close to Krishna because he had loyally stood by him when Krishna was wrongly accused of stealing a precious gem that belonged Satyabhama's (now his wife) father, Satrajit. He had journeyed into the forests near Dwarka to search for the gem. On that journey, Satyaki had fought bravely against the bear king Jambhavan and had been badly injured. His bravery had endeared him to all, especially Krishna and Balarama.

As all the gods led by Lord Brahma and Lord Indra looked on, Krishna using his lethal bow to great effect, unleashed fiery arrows of every kind. They covered the distance between the armies with great ease, conjuring up fire, gale force winds, hailstorms, icy blizzards and hot desert winds. All the ghosts and ghouls who made up a large part of Shiva's army were terrified and ran helter-skelter. Enraged by the cowardly way in which his soldiers had fled, Shiva began to use all his powerful weapons against Krishna.

It was an evenly matched contest between two of the greatest gods of the universe. The Preserver ranged against the Destroyer. Both were able to fiercely counteract the other's weapons. If Shiva endowed an arrow with special powers by chanting some *mantras*, Krishna did the same to bring about the opposite effect. If Shiva's arrow started a violent hurricane on the battlefield, Krishna's arrow brought rain. And as the gods and demi-gods watched from above, the battle between Banasura's armies and the Yadavas fast became a contest between the two great gods.

CHAPTER FIVE

THE COLLISION OF WONDER WEAPONS

The battle raged on, and after a few gruelling days of conflict, Shiva decided to use a most powerful and treasured weapon called the *Pashupataastra*. But Krishna had his own answer to it—the *Narayanaastra*.

When he saw that his most fearsome weapon had little effect on Krishna, Shiva was frustrated and disenchanted. He appeared to lose interest and detached himself from the battlefield. In that moment, Krishna took advantage of the situation. He chanted another *mantra* and shot an arrow that would make its intended target very drowsy. As soon as the arrow brushed past

Shiva, he was overwhelmed with fatigue. He began to yawn and toss his great mane of hair, as he tried vainly to ward away sleep. But he could not fight it. As waves of exhaustion and sleep overcame him, he put down his weapons and decided to rest a while.

Krishna seized the opportunity and turned his attention towards Banasura and his armies. With his weapons, especially the redoubtable *sudarshan chakra*, or spinning disc, he wreaked havoc on Banasura's armies.

Meanwhile Krishna's son, Pradyumna, was engaged in a fierce contest with Kartikeya, the younger son of Shiva. Although he put up a tough fight, Kartikeya was soon injured by a perfectly aimed arrow and had to be carried off the battlefield by his ever-loyal vehicle, the peacock.

Balarama, who was renowned across the universe for his skills with the mace, had no problem overcoming Bana's commander-in-chief, Kumbhanda, with his club. Kupakarna was similarly felled and with both able generals fatally wounded, the rest of Banasura's army found itself in disarray.

Banasura realized that his army was now in total chaos and his commanders had been felled. His anger knew no bounds. He knew he had to check Krishna, or his entire army would be decimated in no time. So turning away from Satyaki, he turned his attention to Krishna. He used his thousand arms to good effect, wielding five hundred bows that sent off a storm of arrows towards Krishna.

But Krishna remained unperturbed. With his *chakra*, he effortlessly sliced off every one of Banasura's bowstrings. And as Banasura advanced swiftly towards him, Krishna shattered his chariot too. Then Krishna stood tall on his chariot and blew loudly and triumphantly on *Panchajanya*, his conch shell. Everyone on the battlefield heard Krishna's sign of victory and the humiliation of Banasura.

However, Banasura had one more card up his sleeve. The *asura* king revered a sorceress called Kotara and she had promised him her protection. Now, seeing him in trouble, she appeared on the scene. She assumed the form of beautiful temptress and tried to distract Krishna. And when he did not pay any attention, she took the form of a shrieking and terrifying demoness, whose cries made those watching tremble and shiver. But Krishna calmly turned his head away and continued with his attack. This moment's respite, however, enabled Banasura to hurriedly escape inside his fortress.

Now Shiva was witness to all this. Once again he remembered the boon he had granted. Now with fresh vigour, he reappeared on the field. This time it was going to be a fight to the finish.

Shiva strode out into the battlefield and released his most fearful and powerful weapon, the *Shivajvara*. The *Shivajvara* wrought its deadly destruction by releasing vast amounts of intense heat. It could send temperatures shooting up, making things twelve times hotter than the sun could, burning up everything in its path. When Shiva unleashed this weapon, it sprouted three heads and three legs and rapidly made its way towards Krishna, scorching the battlefield as it went on.

Krishna though, was ready for it. As Vishnu's avatar, he had a weapon to counter it, called the *Narayanajvara* which contrary to the *Shivajvara*, emanated extreme cold. When Krishna saw Shiva's powerful weapon headed his way, he had no choice but to release the *Narayanajvara*. And as the two weapons moved towards each other, those watching, including the waiting gods, felt a great trepidation and fear, for both weapons were immensely powerful and could wreak great havoc on the universe.

The two weapons collided in the sky and the atmosphere glowed as both released vast amounts of energy. Heat poured forth from Shiva's weapon, only to be doused by a bitterly cold wind. The heat tried to consume everything with its hotness, but a thick cold cover grew over everything. The *Shivajvara* could not subdue the *Narayanjvara* and had no option but to cry for help. It begged for Shiva's intervention, but this time Shiva was powerless to help, for if he took back the weapon, the heat would consume him as well. Ultimately, the *Shivajvara*, finding itself spent and losing its heat, rapidly offered itself up to Krishna. The three-headed weapon bowed low, folding its three arms, and asked Krishna to be his protector.

Hearing the weapon out, Krishna reassured it that the *Narayanajvara* would no longer be of danger to him. 'You have nothing to fear from the *Narayanjvara*,' he told the hapless weapon. 'And I promise that whoever has witnessed this horrific conflict and can recall it later, will be free from fear as well,' he added.

It appeared that the great battle was finally over. Or was it?

CHAPTER SIX

THE DEFEAT OF BANASURA

While this great battle was taking place, Banasura stayed in his palace regaining his strength. Now he returned, rejuvenated and with a will to destroy Krishna. He charged onto the battlefield appearing directly before Krishna, armed with a different weapon in each of his one thousand hands.

He was half-crazed with anger and frustration at the immense losses his armies had suffered. So he lashed out at Krishna with his many weapons—tridents, swords, maces, bows and arrows. Krishna saw these weapons aimed at him and raising his hand, he spun the *sudarshana chakra* and cut off Banasura's arms one after another.

Shiva saw that Banasura was clearly no match for Krishna and his *sudarshana chakra* and that he was losing his arms one by one. He realized that he had to intervene. He appeared in their midst and raised his hand to draw Krishna's attention.

'Krishna, the whole universe knows that you are Vishnu's manifestation and that you have the power to

overlook sins committed in error and in ignorance. I plead with you to save this *asura*'s life. He has been a loyal devotee to me and you had promised Prahlada, his forefather, that you would not harm or kill any of his descendants. I now beg you to spare his life.'

Krishna heard Shiva and then acknowledging his request on behalf of Banasura said, 'I remember very well the promise I had made to Prahlada. I also know he is the son of Bali, a most brave and generous king. And so, I promise not to kill Bana. However, I will destroy his many arms, save four, so that he learns humility and repents his past misdeeds.'

Banasura was immensely relieved and grateful that his life was to be spared. He fell at Krishna's feet, 'O Lord, forgive me! I have let my ambition blind me and cause pain and destruction.' He was also very remorseful for having captured Aniruddha and keeping him prisoner for so long.

He ordered his soldiers to release Aniruddha at once. Then, Banasura seated both Usha and Aniruddha in a chariot and personally escorted them to Krishna. Krishna led the young couple back to Dwarka. All of Dwarka was eagerly waiting to greet the victorious army and the young and beautiful couple. Lamps were lit, flags fluttered and garlands draped homes as the joyous citizens of Dwaraka gave their heroes a grand welcome.

CHAPTER SEVEN

A GODDESS IS BORN TO KILL AN ASURA

There is another legend of Banasura, which describes him as an *asura* who had conquered all the three realms and was virtually invincible. This king mercilessly oppressed his subjects because he knew that no one could oppose him. His confidence and arrogance stemmed from the fact that he had been granted a boon because of which no one could kill him, save a young unmarried girl.

This boon made him stronger than anyone else on earth. No brave warrior could match Banasura. His subjects were in despair. They wondered if they would ever be free from the oppression Banasura inflicted on them. Even Mother Earth was tired of seeing her people suffer and hearing their piteous cries.

She decided to take matters in her own hands and made her way to Vaikuntha, which was Lord Vishnu's abode. She knew that the great Preserver was the only one who would be able to right the balance of the universe. Once there, she folded her hands and appealed to Lord Vishnu, 'O Lord Vishnu,' she said. 'I cannot see my people suffer anymore. Will you not come to their assistance and rid the world of the evil Banasura?' Vishnu heard her out and responded, 'O Great Mother, this *asura* is truly evil and deserves to be punished. However, he is protected by a great boon. Neither I, nor any of the other gods can touch him. I have thought about this and realized that there is a loophole in the boon and if we use that to our advantage, only then Banasura can be defeated. There is one person who can help you and that is the Supreme Goddess Shakti. If you can appease her, she will emerge on earth in the form of a young maiden and destroy the *asura*.

Armed with this bit of good news, Mother Earth went to the other gods in Heaven and together with them performed a great sacrifice. After many years of chanting *mantras* and performing complex rituals, Goddess Shakti emerged from the sacrificial pyre.

'I have come in response to your prayers,' she said. 'What is it that you want of me?' asked the goddess.

The gods bowed in respect and they spoke as a single

body. 'O Great Goddess, we need your help to rid the world of a great evil,' they said. They then described the long years of oppression the world had borne at the hands of Banasura. They mentioned that the arrogance of the asura king knew no bounds and very soon, he would set his sights on Heaven itself unless he was checked.

'So we ask you to take the form of a young unmarried maiden and kill Banasura, because according to the boon, she is the only one who can do so.' begged the gods.

Goddess Shakti, who was actually a manifestation of Goddess Parvati, grew terribly angry upon hearing about Banasura's cruelty. She immediately agreed to help the gods and soon after appeared on earth as Kumari.

Kumari was a beautiful and pure-hearted young maiden. She and settled down in Kanyakumari. Now Kanyakumari was believed to be a very holy place as the waters of the three great oceans met here. Her powers were enhanced by the divinity of the place. To make herself even stronger, she prayed to Lord Shiva, reciting his name over and over, as she meditated on the beach.

Lord Shiva, who lived not too far from Kanyakumari, at a place called Suchindram, had heard about this young goddess who had appeared on earth. He was also impressed by her devotion to him. So one day, he appeared at Kanyakumari and hiding behind a tree, watched the simply dressed young maiden absorbed in her deep meditation.

Kumari's godly beauty and her heavenly glow, even in her simple, earthly avatar, was evident to all. She radiated with her inner strength and Lord Shiva fell in love with her almost immediately.

He appeared in front of the young maiden and said, 'O Goddess, you have won me over with your devotion. Not only do I bless you but I also would like you to be my consort.'

The young maiden blushed despite being a goddess and speechless at the offer from one of the greatest gods in the universe, she simply nodded her head in agreement.

However, while all of this was taking place on Kanyakumari, up in Heaven, the gods were dismayed! If Shakti married Shiva, she wouldn't be an unmarried maiden anymore. All their years of sacrifice and penance would come to nothing and Banasura would continue to live and spread his evil across the three worlds.

It was at this complicated moment that Narada decided to come to the rescue.

He convinced the young goddess that her first responsibility was to rid the world of the *asura* and if she had to give up her own happiness for that, so be it.

In order to continue with the plan, he advised Kumari to ask Shiva for three things to prove his worth. These things should be extremely difficult to procure and if Lord Shiva failed to get even one of them, the wedding would be cancelled.

Now Narada knew that Kumari could not displease Shiva with a refusal, but at the same time, she also had to remain an unmarried maiden in order to vanquish the evil Banasura. For these were the conditions laid down in the boon granted to the demon king.

Thus when Lord Shiva appeared before her with a formal proposal of marriage, Kumari asked him to get her three things within a day: a betel leaf with no veins in it, a coconut without its eyes or the special marks that every coconut has, and a stalk of sugarcane with no stumps.

However Lord Shiva was a supreme god and with a few magic *mantras*, he produced all three.

The marriage date was set and an auspicious hour for the ceremony was found. This hour was just before the day broke. However, if Shiva did not appear before dawn, the moment would have passed and the marriage would never be solemnized.

The day arrived and Shiva left for Kanyakumari at the head of a magnificent marriage procession.

As the gods hung their heads in misery, Narada arrived at a final decision. He had already decided on a new plan and was ready and waiting.

When the procession had almost reached, Narada appeared behind them. He hid behind some bushes and mimicked the crowing of a rooster.

'What? Has the dawn already broken?' said Shiva thunderstruck.

Now the sky had indeed lost its inky blackness of night, but neither was it dawn. It was the magic twilight hour that Narada took full advantage of to fool Shiva and his party.

Convinced that they had somehow missed the ordained hour, Shiva turned back. Everyone was saddened and the marriage between these two gods was never solemnized.

The grand wedding feast was scattered across the sandy beach and it is believed that that over time, they turned into coloured pebbles, sea shells and shingles, which to this day lie on the beach at Kanyakumari!

Now Kumari's fame had spread far and wide. Word reached Banasura and he had also heard of Lord Shiva's failure. Wanting to succeed where a god had failed, Banasura sent Kumari a grand proposal with a train of gifts and servants. He promised her all the riches of the world and every comfort known to man and gods alike.

However, Kumari turned him down and treated all his gifts and overtures with great contempt.

An angry and offended Banasura decided to destroy the proud woman. He marched to Kanyakumari with his army intending to tear the maiden to shreds, but the moment he came face to face with Kumari, he realized that she was no ordinary woman, but a goddess in disguise. He also realized that he was no match for her.

Kumari then, as was ordained, wounded him fatally. As he lay dying, Banasura said, 'O Great Goddess, I seek your forgiveness. Please grant me your pardon before I die.' Kumari did not hesitate. She forgave him, knowing she had fulfilled her mission and rid the universe of this evil *asura*.

Thereafter, Kumari went back to Kanyakumari and resumed her prayers to Shiva, for she had always been devoted to him. It is believed that she continues her penance in the hope of being married to him one day.

MythNotes

Many areas in India are associated with Banasura and there are several sites that could have been his erstwhile capital. In the epic Mahabharata, there is mention of the asura *Bana and his descendants. His progeny came to be known as Banas, and they ruled at a place called Bharatpur in central India. Their capital was at Bayana. The princess of Bayana was Usha who was indeed married to a prince called Aniruddha. There is even a temple at Bayana dedicated to her. It is also said that close to Jabalpur in Madhya Pradesh is Bhere Ghat or Banasura Ghat on the Narmada river, where Banasura meditated and prayed to Shiva.*

However, some suggest that Banasura's kingdom comprised central Assam, and the capital is in present day Tezpur.

Banasura is also associated with the Bamsu Village (now known as Lamgoundi) in the Rudraprayag District of Uttarakhand. This village not only has a temple dedicated to Banasura, who is worshipped as a rain god, but also a smaller one dedicated to Aniruddha. It is said that this village was known in ancient times as Shonitpur, leading many to believe that this village was Sonitapur, Banasura's capital.

There is a hill in the forested Wayanad district of Kerala that is named after Banasura. The Banasura Sagar Dam built close to the hill is the largest earthen dam in India, and also the second largest in Asia.